Also by Gyles Brandreth

Max, the Boy Who Made a Million

Other Collins Red Storybooks

The Enchanted Horse *Magdalen Nabb*
The Dream Snatcher *Kara May*
Whistling Jack *Linda Newbery*
The Puppy Present *Jean Ure*
Abdullah's Butterfly *Janine M. Fraser*
Sasha and the Wolf-Child *Ann Jungman*
Emma's Talking Rabbit *Leon Rosselson*

MAISIE

THE GIRL WHO LOST HER HEAD

GYLES BRANDRETH

Illustrated by John Lupton

CollinsChildren'sBooks

An imprint of HarperCollinsPublishers

519931

First published in Great Britain by Collins in 1999
Collins is an imprint of HarperCollins*Publishers* Ltd
77-85 Fulham Palace Road, Hammersmith, London, W6 8JB

The HarperCollins website address is
www.**fire**and**water**.com

1 3 5 7 9 8 6 4 2

Text copyright © Gyles Brandreth 1999
Illustrations copyright © John Lupton 1999

ISBN 0 00 675296 9

Printed and bound in Great Britain by
Caledonian International Book Manufacturing Ltd,
Glasgow G64

CONTENTS

Chapter One

BEGIN AT THE BEGINNING

My name is Maisie Andrews and this is my story. You are going to find parts of it hard to believe, but every word is true. I promise. Yes, even the bit about meeting the King of England and getting my head chopped off. But that comes later. I'd better begin at the beginning.

I was born on a boat, on the river Thames, on

April Fools' Day in the year 1891. All right, I don't remember much about the day and the year, because I don't remember being born (do you?), but I am certain about the boat. I remember the boat. I loved the boat. I can see it now. I really can.

As I write this, I am looking at a photograph of the boat, our boat, *Noah's Ark*. The photograph is in black and white, but *Noah's Ark* was painted bright yellow and red and green. She – people call boats 'she', don't ask me why – was beautiful. Mum and Dad gave her a new coat of paint every year.

"She's our pride and joy isn't she, Mum?" said Dad.

"She is that, Dad," said Mum.

And she was. *Noah's Ark* was a flat-bottomed barge, about forty feet long and twelve feet wide. In the middle of the deck there was a kind of fixed wooden hut with a pointed shiny black roof and a wooden door (painted green) and eight steep steps like a ladder leading down to three tiny cabins. The main cabin was the kitchen and sitting-room. We called it the galley. Beyond the galley were two narrow cabins with bunk beds in each of them. We called them berths. My mum and dad slept in one and Max and I slept in the other. I'll tell you about Max in a minute.

My dad used to say, "*Noah's Ark* is the finest barge ever to sail the seven seas," which was a silly thing to say because *Noah's Ark* never sailed anywhere. She was moored to a pier just below Hammersmith Bridge. She bobbed up and down when the weather was stormy. She rose and fell in the water as the tide came in and out. But she didn't go anywhere. A hefty rope at one end and an iron anchor at the other kept her in exactly the same spot all the time.

My dad and mum were called Mr and Mrs Noah. That wasn't their real name, of course. That was their stage name. They were clog-dancers.

Clogs were special shoes with wooden soles and when you danced in them on a wooden stage they made the most wonderful sound: clackety-bang, clackety-bang, click, click, clash-crash. Dad and Mum called themselves 'The Champion Clog-Dancers of the World' and they earned their living dancing in theatres and music-halls all over London.

I didn't have any brothers or sisters, but I did have Max and Max was my best friend.

I first set eyes on him on 1 April 1899, my eighth birthday. I'll never forget it. I was sitting in the galley with Mum, drinking lemonade and eating a piece of chocolate birthday cake. Mum was getting cross because Dad had said he was "popping out for half a mo – won't be a tick" – and it was an hour later and he wasn't back yet.

"I don't like to think what nonsense he's getting up to," Mum muttered, shaking her head. "Where is he? Where *is* he?"

"Here I am," said Dad with a laugh, coming down the steep steps. "And look! I've brought company."

"Goodness gracious me!" shrieked Mum, looking up. "What's that? It can't be—"

"It is," grinned Dad.

"It's a monkey!" I jumped up. I was so excited, I couldn't believe my eyes.

"To be accurate, Miss Maisie, he's a marmoset."

He was the most beautiful little animal you ever saw. He was small and brown and very furry, with a long hairy tail that curled around Dad's shoulder and bright brown eyes and lovely fluffy tufts on his ears.

"He's lovely!" I said.

"He's called Max," said Dad, "and he's yours, Maisie. Happy birthday!"

"Oh no," said Mum, burying her face in her hands.

"Oh come on, Mum," said Dad. "Maisie needs a

friend, someone to keep her company when we're out at the theatre at nights."

"Where's he going to sleep?" asked Mum.

"On the bottom bunk," I said, taking the little creature from Dad and holding him in my arms for the first time. He was so sweet and soft and warm.

"Jack Andrews," said Mum sternly (she always called Dad by his real name when she was cross with him), "Jack Andrews, we cannot keep a monkey on a barge."

"He's a marmoset I tell you," said Dad, with a gentle smile. "And if we can't find room for a marmoset on a boat called *Noah's Ark*, I don't know what the world is coming to."

"No, Jack."

"Please, Mum," I begged. "It's my birthday."

Mum sighed. "I don't know what to make of you, Maisie Andrews, losing your head over a scruffy little monkey—"

"But he's so sweet," I said.

"And as I keep telling you, my dear," said Dad, "he's no ordinary monkey. He's a marmoset."

"Oh, I don't know what to say…" Mum shook her head again. I could tell she was going to give in.

"Say 'Yes'," laughed Dad. "Go on."

And he lifted Max out of my arms and took him over to Mum, and Max put a tiny paw up to Mum's face and stroked her cheek and looked up at her with his friendly, twinkly brown eyes.

"Oh, very well," said Mum, smiling at last. "But if he's going to be your monkey, Maisie Andrews, you are going to have to look after him, my girl."

Chapter Two

SATURDAY 9 AUGUST

Max didn't need much looking after. He kept himself clean. He was a tidy eater and, at night, he curled up on his bunk and slept like a baby.

"He's no more than a baby, I don't suppose," said Mum. "How old is he, do you think?"

"I don't know," said Dad. "I think he's full grown. They stay quite small, do marmosets."

Dad had bought him for sevenpence-halfpenny from a South American sailor who, Dad said, "didn't speak a word of English, not a word. And I don't speak no Spanish – nor no Portuguese for that matter – so I don't know how the sailor came by him or where he comes from or anything. All I know is that the moment I saw him I reckoned he was just what my Maisie needed."

"Thanks, Dad!"

It wasn't long before Mum loved Max as much as Dad and I did. Max seemed to go out of his way to please her. He used to run and jump and scamper and swing all over the boat, but he was careful never to get under Mum's feet. At mealtimes, he sat quietly on top of the cupboard in the corner of the galley watching us eat, patiently waiting till Mum took him over his bowl of left-overs.

"I must say," she said, tickling him under the chin, "he's a very well-behaved little monkey."

"He's a marmoset, Mum."

"Whatever he is," said Mum, "he's a bit of a treasure."

We led a simple, happy life in those days. I didn't go to school (Dad didn't believe in school), but every morning I had lessons at home. Mum taught me to write and read (Mum loved reading) and showed me how to do sums and made me learn my times-tables (I hated my times-tables – the eights and the nines were the worst). Dad taught me singing and clog-dancing and fishing (Dad loved to fish).

Every afternoon, after lunch, Max and I set off for a walk. Sometimes we went alone, along the tow-path to the gardens at Fulham Palace or through Hammersmith to the little bluebell wood at the far side of Shepherd's Bush. Sometimes Dad took us across the new suspension bridge, all orange-gold and marrow-green, to fish for trout at Barn Elms. Dad had made a small fishing rod for me for my seventh birthday. Now he made another one, even smaller, for Max and, believe it or not (it's true, I promise), Max caught a fish the first time he tried.

"It's only a tiddler," said Dad, "but it's not bad for a beginner."

"That monkey's taken to fishing like a duck to water," laughed Mum when we got home.

"He's a marmoset, Mum."

"Whatever he is, he's a marvel," said Mum. "Come here you cheeky monkey, let's have a cuddle."

In the evenings, except on Sunday, Mum and Dad went off to work. They set off any time between five and six, soon after tea, and never got back before midnight. They danced in two or three different music-halls every night. And when they went off they left me and Max to guard the boat.

"Look after *Noah's Ark*," said Dad. "She's our pride and joy."

When Mum and Dad were out at work, Max and I never left the barge. In summer, if it was warm, we played games up on the deck. In winter, and when it was cold or wet, we went below deck and I read to Max from one of Mum's books or made up stories to tell him or tried to teach him how to play dominoes (he was much better at fishing than at dominoes). At half-past eight, I tucked him up in his bunk and I climbed into mine, and by nine o'clock we were both fast asleep.

Yes, it was a simple and a happy life. Until the day came when the terrible fire changed everything.

The day was Saturday 9 August in the year 1902. It was a special day throughout the land because it was the day of the coronation of the new king. "Fat King Edward," Dad called him.

"Jack Andrews, that's no way to speak of the King," said Mum sternly. Dad laughed.

The day of the coronation was a public holiday, a day for processions and parades, street parties, funfairs and firework displays. "Nobody has to work today," said Dad, "except your mum and me. We're doing four shows tonight in four different halls – but we're getting extra money. Long live the King!"

After lunch, Mum and Dad decided to have a snooze and Max and I went off for our walk. We dressed Max in a special coronation suit that Mum had made from a piece of red velvet curtain. It had a lovely white lace collar and cuffs.

"He looks like a little prince," said Mum.

"And you look like a little princess," said Dad, kissing me on the head. "Be careful how you go now. There'll be crowds and crowds about today."

There were. Everywhere we walked, the streets were full of happy, smiling people, laughing, cheering, drinking, dancing, waving flags, singing "God save the King" and "For he's a jolly good fellow". We walked for miles. I don't know where we went because, of course, we got lost. It didn't seem to matter because everyone was friendly, and I knew I could never get really lost in London. All I needed to do was find the river and walk along it and eventually I'd be home.

We must have walked for four whole hours because we didn't get back to Hammersmith Bridge till nearly six o'clock. And when we did, what we saw was so terrible – so dreadful – so horrible – that even now, years and years later, writing about it is making my heart break all over again.

I cannot put it in my own words, but you need to know what happened, so read this. It is the newspaper report that appeared three days later in the London Evening Star:

CORONATION DAY ACCIDENT

A Coronation Day firework display ended in tragedy on Saturday night when a giant rocket was accidentally launched from Hammersmith Bridge and landed on a barge moored below, setting it alight. The barge instantly burst into flames and the heat was so intense that firefighters who arrived on the scene within minutes were unable to board the vessel in time to rescue the owners.

The small barge, which was completely destroyed in the fire, was the *Noah's Ark*, a colourful and familiar sight to river-users on that stretch of the Thames. The owners, who lost their lives in the blaze, were Mr and Mrs Jack Andrews, better known to the public as the music-hall artistes 'Mr and Mrs Noah, Clog-Dancing Champions of the World.'

Chapter Three

"NO! NO! NO!"

The rest of that terrible day is just a blur to me now. I remember the smell of burning wood and the yellow smoke rising from the water. I remember the silent crowd standing watching as one of the firefighters came and put his arm around me and took me over to a policeman who took my hand and said, "I'm sorry about this, little lady." I remember hugging Max to me so tight that I could feel his little heart beating against mine. I remember feeling numb and empty and alone. I remember I was too unhappy to cry.

The policeman was a kind man, with red cheeks and a ginger moustache. He told me he was called PC Rogers. He took me to Hammersmith Police Station and sat me on the counter and took out his pencil and notebook and said, "Now, little lady, have you got any brothers or sisters?"

"No," I replied.

"Any aunties or uncles you could stay with?"

"No."

"Any grandpa or grandma or that sort of thing?"

"No."

PC Rogers took off his helmet and scratched his head and said, "What about friends?"

"I've got Max."

The police sergeant standing behind PC Rogers

laughed and said, "He's a monkey, isn't he?"

"He's a marmoset," I said, squeezing Max close to me.

"Where do you go to school, little lady?" asked PC Rogers.

"I don't go to school," I said.

PC Rogers sucked on his pencil. "Oh dearie me," he sighed. "What are we going to do with you, little lady? Well, I suppose while we get you sorted out you'd better come home with me. Your marmo-whatever-he's-called will be a nice surprise for Mrs Rogers."

I stayed with the policeman and his wife for nearly three weeks. They were very kind to me. They found me clothes and gave me food and let me sleep in their sitting room, by the fireside, curled up on the sofa under an old blanket, with Max at my side.

One evening PC Rogers came home from work looking very pleased with himself.

"Good news," he announced. "We've got you sorted, little lady. Wait for it… you're going to Canada!"

"I don't want to go to Canada," I shouted. "I don't know where Canada is. Why am I going to Canada?"

"Canada is here," said PC Rogers with a smile, spinning the small globe that sat on the sideboard and showing me a country on the other side of the world. "And when you get to Canada, little lady, you can start a new life – with a new family. There are nice people in Canada who haven't got children of their own and want to adopt lovely little girls like you."

For the first time since the night of the accident, I burst into tears.

"Now don't cry, little lady. Trust me. It's all for the best."

I knew it was all for the worst on the day Mr and Mrs Rogers took me to the railway station to catch the train to Liverpool to take the boat to Canada.

"I don't want to go, I don't want to go," I kept repeating as the police carriage drove us across London.

"You say that now, little lady, but you wait and see. Canada's a wonderful place. It's the land of opportunity. Everybody says so."

At the ticket barrier at Euston station I said goodbye to Mrs Rogers and thanked her for the clothes and the suitcase she had given me.

"That's all right, dear," she said, and when she leant over to kiss me I saw she had tears in her eyes. "And you'll see I've packed you a nice cheese sandwich and an orange and a little piece of chocolate. Don't eat it all at once."

PC Rogers walked along the platform with me carrying my case. "This is the Liverpool train," he said, "And if I'm not much mistaken, this here is your carriage."

He opened the carriage door and helped me in. "Look," he said, "there's another little lady already here. Are you on your way to Canada too?"

"Yes," whispered the girl, who was smartly dressed in a navy-blue jacket and had lovely red hair and not-so-lovely red eyes. She had been crying too.

"Now," said PC Rogers, "you two girls make friends. At every stop there'll be a policeman on the platform to check you're all right, and when you get to Liverpool you'll find there's another policeman, Sergeant Forrest, waiting to meet you. He'll take you across town to the docks. This time tomorrow you'll be on the *SS Discovery*. It's going to be a great adventure."

On the platform the guard blew his whistle and waved his green flag. PC Rogers patted me gently on the head and said, "Goodbye now, little lady, and good luck."

And as he began to step out of the carriage on to

the platform, he suddenly leaned towards me and grabbed Max out of my arms.

"No," I screamed, "no! Give him back!"

"You can't take him with you, little lady. I'm sorry. He'll be all right. Don't worry. We'll send him to the zoo. He'll be fine."

The policeman pushed the carriage door shut and stepped back as the train lurched forward.

"No, no, no!" I cried, "Max! Max, don't go!"

The train wheezed and hissed and clattered its way out of the station and Max and PC Rogers disappeared in a cloud of steam.

I fell back into the carriage and I sobbed my heart out. I had lost everybody now.

The girl with the red hair and the red eyes came and sat next to me. "What was he called, your monkey?" she asked.

"He's a marmoset," I sobbed. "He's called Max."

"That's a nice name," said the girl very softly.

"My name's Kate and I'm an orphan. How do you do?"

"How do you do?" I said through my tears. "My name's Maisie and I'm an orphan too."

Kate lent me her hankie to dry my eyes and blow my nose and, as the train raced northwards, through my sniffles and sobs I told her my story. I told her all about Mum and Dad and the *Noah's Ark* and the terrible fire. And when I had told her my story, she told me hers. She had never known her father, and her mother had died when she was born. She had been brought up by her only grandmother and now she had died too, and so Kate, like me, was being sent to Canada to be adopted by a new family.

"I don't want to go to Canada," she said. "Do you?"

"Of course not!" I cried. "I want to live on a boat on the river Thames, that's what I want to do."

"I'd love to live on a boat," said Kate.

"You can come and live on my boat," I said.

"But you haven't got a boat," said Kate sadly. "Oh dear, what can we do?"

"We can run away," I said, all of a sudden. "We can escape! That's what we can do."

"We can't," said Kate.

"We can. Why not? We can look after ourselves. I can get a job. I can sing and clog-dance and fish."

"And I can sew," said Kate, her eyes widening.

"There you are!" I said, and I almost laughed.

"But how are we going to escape? You heard what he said. There's going to be a policeman at every station – and we can't jump off a moving train."

"Can't we?" I said, and I stood up and went over to the carriage window. I looked out and I couldn't believe my eyes. Guess what I saw?

Chapter Four

"JUMP, KATE, JUMP!"

"It's a monkey's tail!" squealed Kate.

"It's a marmoset's tail, silly!" I shouted, bursting into tears all over again. "It's Max! He must have managed to escape as the train was leaving the station – and he's been riding on the roof. Isn't he brilliant?"

Carefully I lowered the carriage window and

reached out. Max was clinging to the side of the train, but the moment he saw me he swung down towards the open window and climbed in. I hugged him so hard I made him squeak. Then I introduced him to Kate.

"Max, this is Kate. Kate, this is Max."

Kate looked a little nervous, but she shook his outstretched paw. "How do you do?" she said, quite formally.

I laughed. I was happy again. "He doesn't speak," I explained, "but he understands everything. He's very clean and tidy. And very, very clever. He catches fish. He can do everything. Except he's no good at dominoes. Oh," – and I hugged him hard – "and he's my best *best* friend."

"I wish I had a best friend," said Kate, rather sadly.

"You have, silly!" I laughed again. "You've got two now. Here we are. And we're going to run away together and makes lots of money and live on a boat and—"

Just then the train juddered to a complete standstill.

"Where are we?" I asked.

"I don't know."

"We aren't anywhere," I said, staring out of the open carriage window. "Look."

The train had stopped in the middle of nowhere. All you could see out of the window were green and yellow fields and, on the horizon, a clutch of tiny cottages. We were somewhere in the countryside, but I had no idea where.

I was excited. I turned to Kate. "Look, it's a meadow full of buttercups – and there's a cow. Let's do it. Let's get off – here and now. Come on!"

"What if it's a bull?" Kate stammered.

"It isn't a bull, silly. It's a cow. Come on. Now's our chance!"

I threw open the door of the carriage and looked down on to the meadow. It was a long drop. Out loud I counted, "One – two – three" – and I jumped.

I tumbled on to the grass and rolled over and over again. I picked myself up and turned back towards the train and called up to Kate and Max. "I've made it. Come on! Hurry!"

Max jumped next. It was an easy jump for a marmoset.

"Don't forget the suitcases," I shouted. "I want my cheese sandwich and my chocolate!"

Kate threw me my suitcase.

"Come on, Kate," I called. "You next. Come on, jump!"

"I'm scared."

"Don't be, silly."

"Are you sure it isn't a bull?"

"Jump, Kate, jump!"

But it was too late. Suddenly, with a tremendous judder, the train began to move again. The carriage door slammed shut. The train thundered off down the track and disappeared. No sooner had I met my new friend Kate than she was gone.

I didn't have time to think about what to do next because, as I turned round to pick up my suitcase, I felt a hand on my shoulder. I gave a yelp and looked up and found myself gazing into the face of a funny-looking little old man.

"Hello, hello, hello," he said in a strange-sounding voice, "what's going on here?"

I didn't know what to say. The little old man looked very old and very odd, but he seemed quite friendly. He smiled at me and I saw that in his mouth he only had one tooth. It was bright yellow and stuck out over his lower lip.

"What are you doing in my field with your monkey frightening my bull?" he asked.

"He's a marmoset."

"Is he now? And you're the Queen of Sheba, I suppose."

"No," I said, "I'm Maisie Andrews and I'm – I'm – "

"Looking for the road to Rugby, are you?"

"No," I said. "As a matter of fact, I'm looking for a job."

"Oh, are you now?" said the funny-looking little old man. "What can you do?"

"I can sing," I began. "And I can clog-dance. And I can fish."

"There's not a lot of call for singing and clog-dancing in these parts," he said with a chuckle, and as he laughed his tooth seemed to wobble. "And, as a rule, I does my own fishing. But, strange as it may seem, I likes the look of you, and we haven't had a monkey on the farm before, so I'll help you if I can."

"Thank you," I said. "Thank you very much."

The funny-looking little old man gave a little laugh. "Have you run away from home?" he asked.

"I haven't got a home," I said. "All I've got is Max."

"You haven't got a home," he repeated, lifting his hat and scratching his funny bald head. "How come?"

He was certainly very odd to look at, but there was something about him I liked. I felt I could trust him. I told him my story – about Mum and Dad and *Noah's Ark* and the terrible fire, about PC Rogers and going to Canada, about taking the train to Liverpool and the police being at every station, about meeting Kate, and finding Max again, and jumping off the train.

"That's quite a story," he said when I had finished. He scratched his head again and sucked his tooth and looked at me and then at Max and then at me again.

"I'll tell you what we'll do," he said at last. "We'll strike a bargain. If any policemen come here looking for a girl and a monkey I'll tell them I haven't seen any such thing – and I haven't – "

"Because he isn't a monkey, he's a marmoset!"

"Exactly," chuckled my funny-looking friend. "But I think you should send that PC Rogers and his Mrs a postcard telling them you're safe and sound. We don't want them worrying about you, do we now? Agreed?"

"Agreed."

"Good. Now I'd better introduce myself. I'm Farmer Walter."

"And I'm Maisie Andrews."

"Pleased to meet you, Maisie. You say you're looking for a job, eh? How do you fancy picking cabbages? There's a penny a day and all found."

And that's how it happened. Within an hour of jumping off to the train to Liverpool I found myself in Farmer Walter's cabbage field, picking cabbages for a penny a day and all found.

It turned out 'all found' meant that I could eat breakfast and tea with the other farmworkers and, at night, I could sleep safely under cover in the big barn where my farmer friend stored his hay. Max loved life on the farm. In the evening he loved hiding in the bales of hay and jumping and swinging himself around the rafters of the big barn. During the day, when he wasn't helping me in the field, he was making friends with the animals.

"He's a funny little fellow, your marmoset," said the farmer, "and no mistake."

The big cabbage field where I worked was at the far side of the farm, by the main road leading to the nearest town, a place called Rugby. Several times a day carriages trundled down the road, and whenever I heard one coming I tried to hide between the rows of cabbages. I didn't want anyone to find me and take me away and send me off to Canada. But hiding in a field of cabbages isn't easy – especially when you've got a marmoset running about around you. When people in the carriages caught sight of Max they used to laugh and call out to us and wave.

One day, when we had been on the farm for nearly a month, I was out in the field on my own when a carriage drove past and I heard a man's loud voice shout, "Whoa, coachman! Whoa!"

The carriage pulled to a halt. I threw myself on to the ground and crawled along the row of cabbages. My heart was thumping. From behind the largest, leafiest cabbage I could find, I looked out and saw a very tall thin man with a very long thin face stepping slowly down from the carriage. He wore a shiny black top hat and a beautiful dark green cape. In his hand he held a silver-topped cane.

He walked to the edge of the field and called out to me, "You there, kindly step forward."

"Who? Me?" I stammered.

"Who else, child?" he barked, looking around the empty field. "You've got exactly what I am looking for."

"Have I?" I didn't know what he was talking about.

"Cabbages! I need lots of cabbages. How much are they?"

Suddenly I felt safe again. "They're a farthing each, sir," I said quickly.

"Good," said the tall thin stranger, clapping his hands, "I'll have two dozen then."

"So you're not a policeman?" I asked.

"Of course not." He sounded amazed. "Do I look like a policeman?" He pushed his face down towards mine. "Don't you know who I am, child? Don't you recognise me? I am world-famous!"

"Are you?" I stuttered.

"I am," he thundered. "I am the Great Zapristi!"

Chapter Five

THE MASTER OF ILLUSION

The Great Zapristi lifted his hat, threw back his cape and bowed. He was so grand I felt I ought to curtsey, but I didn't know how to curtsey then, so instead, I said, "How do you do?" and put out my hand, expecting him to shake it.

He didn't. Very slowly he lifted it to his lips, gently kissed my fingers and said, "Enchanted to meet you, child!"

Then he dropped my hand and sighed and looked around the field again and, shaking his head sadly, said, "I suppose I should not be surprised that my reputation has not reached this rustic backwater, but I am disappointed all the same. In truth, I have been disappointed ever since I arrived in England. I come from the United States of America. Believe me, I am world-famous there." He gave another bow and pointed to the horse-drawn carriage with his cane. "I take it you will not be travelling to Rugby to see me?"

"What do you do?" I asked.

"What do I do?" he exploded. "What do I do?" He held his arms out wide. "Can you not tell? Is it not obvious? I am the Great Zapristi, the man of a million secrets, the master of illusion! I am a magician, child. I can turn this" – and as he spoke he threw his silver-topped cane into the air – "into this!" And as he caught the cane, suddenly it turned into a beautiful bunch of brightly-coloured flowers.

I clapped my hands. "That's wonderful," I said, laughing, "but if you don't mind my asking, why does the master of illusion need two dozen cabbages?"

"Can't you guess?"

"No," I said.

"They are an essential part of my act." He looked at me very seriously. "You see, I chop off people's heads."

"With cabbages?"

"Don't be ridiculous, child! I chop off people's heads with a silver blade that's razor-sharp. And to prove how razor-sharp it is, before I chop off a real head, I chop up a few cabbages. It's called 'building the tension'. Since I arrived in your country I must have played in every theatre and music-hall in the land and, though I say it myself, there is not a finer magic act to be seen anywhere. The audiences adore me!"

"Did you know my Mum and Dad?" I asked.

The Great Zapristi looked surprised. "No, I don't think so. Why should I? I am not in the habit of spending time with farming folk."

"No, I don't come from the country. I'm from London. My Mum and Dad were Mr and Mrs Noah."

It was the Great Zapristi's turn to clap his hands. "Mr and Mrs Noah?" he exclaimed. "The Champion Clog-Dancers of the World?"

I nodded.

He beamed at me. "Mr and Mrs Noah – wonderful people, fine artistes – and you are their child? I should have recognised you at once." He took my hand again and kissed my fingers once more. "I heard about the terrible fire. I am so sorry. I knew your parents well. They were my friends. Look, look—"

And, suddenly, from a deep pocket inside his cape, he produced a small leather wallet. "This is where I keep my special bits and pieces," he said. "My passport, this lock of mermaid's hair – well, she wasn't exactly a mermaid, but I was very fond of her – and here, see, this photograph of your parents. They gave it to me when we appeared together last Christmas."

It was a photograph of Mum and Dad in their stage costumes, and on the picture Dad had written, in his large loopy handwriting, 'To our friend the Great Zapristi, with every good wish for the festive season, from Jack and Rose, Mr and Mrs Noah, Champion Clog-Dancers of the World.'

My eyes blurred with tears. "It's a lovely picture," I managed to say.

"It is," said Zapristi kindly. "They were lovely people."

He stood back to inspect me. "And you, child, are their lovely daughter. They had high hopes for you. I think they hoped you would follow them on to the stage. May I ask what you are doing in this field?"

"Picking cabbages."

"Yes," he said slowly, "but why?"

"I am running away," I said.

"Running away? From what?"

"From the police."

"From the police?" he repeated.

"They want to send me to Canada to be adopted," I said, "but I want to stay in England."

"Of course you do," he roared. "And you shall! The Great Zapristi says so." He tapped the side of his shiny black top hat and smiled. "I have an idea. Tell me, child, what is the farmer paying you for gathering up his cabbages?"

"A penny a day and all found."

"Come with me and I shall give you threepence a day and all found. And what is more, I shall throw knives at you, I shall saw you in half, I shall chop off your head. Doesn't that sound fun?"

"I'm not sure—" I stammered.

"Not sure? Of course you're sure. The daughter

of Mr and Mrs Noah was destined for a life on the stage. I take it you can sing? And, naturally, you can dance." He thought for a moment. "I seem to remember that your name is Maisie."

"That's right."

"I shall make you a princess, Maisie. Come with me and you too can be world-famous. I can see the posters already. 'The Great Zapristi proudly presents his new assistant... The Princess Maisie'!"

"Can I bring Max?"

"Who's Max?" The Great Zapristi narrowed his eyes and looked at me suspiciously.

"My marmoset," I said.

"A monkey! A monkey!" The Great Zapristi was overcome with joy. "A monkey is exactly what I have been looking for. Lead me to him!"

He turned and called back to the carriage that was still waiting at the roadside. "Coachman, I will return in just a moment. Prepare for two more passengers – a princess and her monkey."

"He's a marmoset."

"Whatever you say, Princess. Just lead me to him."

Chapter Six

THE HAPPY HENDERSONS

Right from the start, the Great Zapristi took to Max and Max took to the Great Zapristi. From the moment they met they were friends.

In some ways Max and I were sad to leave the farm. The funny-looking one-toothed farmer and his wife had been very good to me, and Max loved playing in the barn and making friends with the other animals. But I knew we could not go on living on the farm forever. Farmer Walter had already told me he wasn't sure there would be a job for me once the cabbage-picking season was over. And I liked the idea of working as Princess Maisie, the Great Zapristi's new assistant. I suppose he did look a bit frightening in his tall top hat and flowing cape, but in fact Zapristi wasn't frightening at all. He was friendly and funny and kind. And best of all, he had known Mum and Dad. He was their friend. When I was with him I felt close to them again, and I liked that.

The Great Zapristi was touring the country with a troupe of entertainers called 'The Happy Hendersons'.

"There's nothing happy about them," said Zapristi. "They're a miserable lot. And 'Jolly Jim' Henderson is the worst. I don't like him and I don't trust him."

"Why not?"

"I don't know. He doesn't smell right to me."

'Jolly Jim' Henderson didn't smell right to me either. He smelt of tobacco and old socks. He was very fat and when he was on stage, telling his jokes or singing one of his silly songs, he laughed a lot. Off-stage he never laughed at all.

The Happy Hendersons were the stars of our show. It turned out they were quite famous. "It's gone to their heads, I'm afraid," said Zapristi. "Mabel Henderson isn't a bad singer in her way, and those two boys of theirs are fairly good as jugglers go, but why they are as famous as they are beats me. 'Jolly Jim' Henderson is the unfunniest funny man I've ever seen."

One of the reasons the Great Zapristi didn't like him, of course, was that 'Jolly Jim' Henderson was in charge. He was the boss. He paid Zapristi ("I'm giving you more than you're worth, Zapristi, and no mistake!"). He told Zapristi how long he could have on stage ("A quarter of an hour tonight,

Zapristi, not a minute more. D'you understand?").
He was rude to Zapristi ("Mark my words,
Zapristi. You need to sharpen up your act if you
want to go on touring with The Happy
Hendersons.").

Zapristi didn't want to go on touring with The
Happy Hendersons. He wanted to go back to
America. "But I can't afford the fare, so while I
save up, here I am and here I stay." Zapristi didn't
like working with The Happy Hendersons, but he
did like working – he loved being a magician – and
I think it is true to say he liked working with Max
and me.

We quickly became part of his magic act. For his
first illusion the Great Zapristi turned an elephant
into a monkey. Or rather, when a light flashed on
stage, he collapsed a gigantic cardboard cut-out of
an African elephant called Jumbo and revealed a
real South American marmoset called Max. For his
next trick, he brought me on as Princess Maisie and

made me disappear inside 'Zapristi's Magic Chinese Cabinet'. (The 'cabinet' was a simple wooden cupboard with a false back. The moment Zapristi shut the cupboard doors, I slipped out of the back and vanished behind a black curtain.) Finally he made me reappear (with a little help from Max, who pulled back the curtain and then ran around the stage waving a Union Jack) and made the audience clap and cheer while, to a roll of drums, he cut off my head!

The head-chopping trick was an easy one. Zapristi had a special machine that he called a 'guillotine'. It had a steel blade at the top and a wooden block at the bottom and I had to put my head between the two. To show the audience how sharp the blade was, Zapristi put a cabbage where my head was going to go and then, on the count of three, pressed the blade right through the cabbage. With a scrunch and a clunk, the razor-sharp blade chopped the cabbage neatly in two. A moment later, when my head went into the guillotine, the audience always gasped. But there was nothing for me to worry about. Before he pressed down the blade, Zapristi flicked a tiny hidden switch at the back of the machine. The switch blocked the real blade and what came down and seemed to cut through my neck was a second blade, a false one, that had two ends but nothing in the middle.

The Great Zapristi didn't like The Happy Hendersons, but the audiences did. The audiences liked the Great Zapristi too. There was always a big cheer when the time came for Zapristi and Max and me to take our bow.

"We're a good team," said Zapristi. "You're my kind of princess, Maisie, and Max is a marvel. Did I tell you I had another assistant called Max once upon a time? Of course, he was a boy not a monkey. I taught him to walk the tightrope. Only look ahead, never look back. That's the secret of walking the tightrope. That's the secret of life really."

For nearly a year we travelled the length and breadth of England. We went everywhere, from Southampton in the South to Newcastle in the North.

One Saturday evening, when we were somewhere in the middle of England, Zapristi came into our dressing room in a state of great excitement. "Child, there's been a change of plan," he announced. "This time next week we will not be where we thought we'd be. We will not even be in a theatre!"

"Where will we be?" I asked.

"In a castle," said Zapristi, smacking his lips with delight. "A very special castle, as it happens."

"Really?"

"Yes, really. Believe it or not, child, we are on our way to Windsor Castle!"

My heart began to thump. "Isn't that where the King lives?"

"It is," said Zapristi, clapping his hands.

"And are we going to put on a show for the King?"

"We are."

"I don't believe it!"

"But it's true. 'Jolly Jim' Henderson has just given me the news. It seems The Happy Hendersons are favourites with His Majesty. Don't ask me why. There's no accounting for taste. The point is that next Saturday night we are to present an entire show for His Majesty the King and his family and their guests. It is a Royal Command Performance."

"Goodness gracious me," I gasped.

"First thing in the morning, we shall start to rehearse. The Great Zapristi is going to give His Majesty an evening he will never forget!"

Chapter Seven

"OFF WITH HER HEAD!"

It turned out to be an evening nobody would forget. Nobody could. It was amazing.

Windsor Castle is an fantastic place. With its battlements and turrets and towers it looks just like you want a castle to look.

We put on our show in what was called the small ballroom. It was the biggest room you ever saw. It was high and wide and incredible. The floor was made of polished wood, so shiny you could see your face in it. The walls were covered with huge mirrors framed with gold. We performed on a low stage specially set up for us at one end of the room, and the King and the Queen and their family and guests sat on red-velvet-covered chairs immediately in front of us. They were so close you could almost touch them.

The King sat right in the middle. I could see why dad had called him Fat King Edward. He was as round as 'Jolly Jim' Henderson. The Queen sat on his right, and around them sat their children and their grandchildren and royal courtiers and royal guests, princes and princesses, dukes and duchesses, marquesses and earls. The gentlemen were all dressed up in evening clothes, wearing white bow ties and black tail coats with carnations in their button-holes. The ladies all looked so beautiful and every one of them was wearing a crown.

Zapristi whispered to me, "Those charming crowns the ladies are wearing are called tiaras. They're lovely, aren't they? They're covered in precious stones. And each one is worth a fortune."

"A fortune," echoed 'Jolly Jim' Henderson, who was standing near us waiting to make his grand entrance.

The show began at exactly seven o'clock. It was different from our normal show. For this one special night 'Jolly Jim' had decided to stay on stage throughout the performance and introduce every act.

Zapristi and Max and I stood at the back of the stage hidden behind a curtain, waiting our turn.

"Your Majesty," 'Jolly Jim' Henderson began, facing the King and bowing as low as his fat tummy would allow him. "Your Majesty," he repeated, bowing almost as low towards the Queen. "Your Royal Highnesses," he bowed a third time. "My lords, ladies and gentlemen," he went on, bowing once more. "The Happy Hendersons have never been happier!"

"Oh get on with it!" hissed Zapristi from behind the curtain.

"What was that?" said the King.

"Nothing, Your Majesty," boomed 'Jolly Jim', "Nothing at all. We're here to entertain you!"

"Get on with it then," muttered Zapristi.

And get on with it he did. For what seemed like half an hour or more, 'Jolly Jim' Henderson told all his funny stories and sang all his silly songs, and to the Great Zapristi's great disgust, the King laughed and laughed and laughed.

When 'Jolly Jim' had finished his turn, he brought his sons on to the stage to do a bit of juggling. Then 'Jolly Jim' introduced Mrs Henderson, who came on and sang a serious song. The King didn't laugh while Mrs Henderson was singing, but he coughed quite a lot. Then 'Jolly Jim' told a few more stories and pulled a funny hat out of the little round suitcase he carried with him everywhere ('Jolly Jim's Jolly Funny Hat Box' he called it) and, wearing his funny hat, 'Jolly Jim' made the King laugh even louder than before.

"He is jolly funny," said the King and, because he was the King, everybody agreed.

At long last it was our turn.

"Your Majesty," boomed 'Jolly Jim', "We now present an act that's a little bit different. I grant you it's not to everyone's taste and it may not be quite up to the highest standards of The Happy Hendersons, but for those that likes magic it isn't too bad. Kindly welcome the Great Zapristi, as he calls himself, with his two assistants, Princess Maisie and Max the monkey!"

On we went, and, as we reached the middle of the stage, the King leaned forward, pointing to Max, and said, "That's no ordinary monkey. That's a marmoset!"

Well, as you can imagine, after that I decided the

King of England could do no wrong. Clearly His Majesty had a soft spot for marmosets in general and Max in particular. Everything Max did made the King laugh. And everything I did seemed to please the King as well. When we got to the trick where Zapristi sliced the cabbages in two and then put my head into the guillotine, the King called out, "Can I say 'Off with her head'?"

"By all means, Your Majesty," said Zapristi, with a bow.

"Thank you," chuckled the King, "I've wanted to do this all my life." The King of England looked at me and winked. "Are you ready, my dear?"

"Yes, Your Majesty," I said.

"Right-o," laughed the King. "Off with her head!"

And swoosh, clunk, down came the false blade. For a moment, the King looked quite alarmed.

"Are you all right, my dear?" he asked.

"I'm fine, Your Majesty," I said with a grin.

Zapristi released me from the guillotine and, together, we took a bow.

"And now," declared Zapristi, swirling his cape around him, "for my final illusion I wish to attempt a feat of magic never seen on any stage before. I call this fantastic feast of prestidigitation 'The Disappearing Crown Jewels'."

The King chuckled. "This sounds promising."

Zapristi continued, "Your Majesty, to assist me with this illusion, I would appreciate the loan of a piece of royal jewellery – a ring or a necklace or a crown."

The King chortled, "Excellent, excellent! I'll give you a ring." He struggled to pull a ring off one of his fat fingers. He pulled and he pulled, but the ring wouldn't budge. He turned to the Princess Royal who was sitting on his left and said, "Louise, give him one of yours – or, better still, let him have little Alexandra's tiara."

'Little Alexandra' turned out to be the King's

granddaughter. She was about my age and very pretty, and she was wearing the most beautiful little crown covered with shining, sparkling diamonds.

"This is fun," she said, getting up and coming to the edge of the stage. "Here, take it." She lifted off the tiara and gave it to me.

Holding it ever so carefully, I took it to Zapristi, who held it up high for everyone to see.

"Your Majesties, Your Royal Highnesses, my lords, ladies, gentlemen," he said. "Watch closely as I place the crown inside my Magic Chinese Cabinet."

'Jolly Jim' Henderson helped me and Max push the cabinet to the centre of the stage. The Great Zapristi opened the cabinet's doors to show the audience it was quite empty. Then he turned to them and said, "A moment ago, you saw my young assistant lose her head. Now we shall see her lose the crown jewels!"

Zapristi handed me the little princess's beautiful tiara and told me to place it inside the cabinet. "Now you see it," he said, closing the cabinet doors, "Abracadabra-cadabra-aboul – Zapristi-capristi-soda-and-whisky – now you don't!" With a flourish he pulled open the cabinet doors and, sure enough, the tiara had disappeared.

The King cried "Bravo!" and everybody cheered. The Great Zapristi took a bow.

The trick was a simple one. While Zapristi was distracting the audience with his swirling cape and his 'Abracadabras' at the front of the stage, I was supposed to slip behind the cabinet and use the cabinet's false back to reach inside and take the tiara. That's what I tried to do – that's what I had practised doing three times a day for a whole week – but, on the night, it turned out I couldn't take the tiara because, when I put my hand inside the cabinet, the tiara had already gone!

Suddenly I heard Zapristi declaring proudly,

"And now Your Majesty, I will make the crown jewels reappear – not only inside the cabinet but on the head of my own princess, my young assistant, Princess Maisie. Abracadabra-cadabra-aboul!"

And with another flourish, Zapristi threw open the cabinet doors. The audience gasped. The cupboard was bare.

"Child," screeched Zapristi, "what's happened?"

"The tiara," I cried. "It's gone, it's really gone! It's disappeared!"

Chapter Eight

"ARREST THAT MAN!"

"Arrest that man! Don't let him escape!" 'Jolly Jim' Henderson was standing at the side of the stage, pointing at Zapristi and shouting, "Arrest him! Arrest him! Don't let him escape!"

Zapristi wasn't trying to escape. He was standing quite still staring into the empty cabinet, his long thin face as white as a sheet.

'Jolly Jim' Henderson's round fat face

meanwhile was bright red and covered in sweat. He turned towards the King and wailed, "Oh, Your Majesty, Your Majesty, the shame of it, the disgrace!" And he suddenly fell on to his knees and burst into tears.

The King stood up. "Hold on, Henderson, don't get carried away. I'm sure it's just a misunderstanding. The tiara can't have gone far. Mr Zapristi will tell us where it is, won't you Mr Zapristi?" The King smiled at poor Zapristi, whose pale white face now seemed to be turning green. "Come on now. Where's the tiara got to, Mr Zapristi?"

Zapristi hung his head. "I'm afraid I don't know," he said sadly, "I really don't know."

"Oh dear," said the Queen, who hadn't spoken before.

"Oh gracious," said the Princess Royal.

"Oh—" began the little princess, and she started to cry.

"Don't you start blubbing," said the King sternly. "It's bad enough having Henderson in tears. It's only a tiara—"

"But it's worth *thousands*," squealed the Princess Royal.

"Then I shall give a reward of a hundred pounds to whoever finds it," said the King. "It can't have gone far."

He turned to two very tall guards who were standing near the door and said, "Guards, take the magician and his assistants to the guard room, search all their belongings and find me that tiara. Henderson, get up off your knees and get along to the kitchen for your supper. I am taking my guests off to dinner now. I shall return at ten o'clock, and if little Alexandra's precious tiara hasn't turned up by then there'll be trouble. Is that understood?"

"Yes, Your Majesty," said everybody all at once.

"Good," said the King. "It's dinner-time. I'm hungry."

The King turned and marched out of the room, followed by the Queen and the tearful princess and all the rest of the royal party.

A footman stepped forward and said to the unhappy Happy Hendersons, "This way to the servants' hall. Follow me."

The two tall guards stepped on to the stage and said to Zapristi and me, "This way to the guard room, you two. We'll carry the cabinet. Bring all your bits and pieces. That includes the monkey."

I didn't have the heart to say, "But he's a marmoset."

In the guardroom Zapristi sat on a bench gazing at the floor, shaking his head and muttering to himself, "I just don't understand."

The two tall guards searched all our bags and baggage. They looked through every case, they opened every box, they brought in Zapristi's Magic Chinese Cabinet and examined every inch of it, inside and out. They searched Zapristi's clothes. They looked inside his hat, they made him empty all his pockets, they even unstitched the silk lining of his beautiful green cloak.

"No sign of it anywhere," said one of them.

"We haven't searched the girl yet," said the other.

"You're right. We'd better search the girl. I'll go and get one of the maids to help."

The taller of the two tall guards went off to find a ladies' maid. Five minutes later he was back, and who do you think he brought with him? A pretty girl with long red hair who I thought I'd never see again. It was Kate! It really was.

"Maisie!" she exclaimed. "I don't believe it!"

"Kate!" I cried, and I ran towards her.

"Not so fast!" barked one of the guards. "You two know each other, do you? Well, there'll be plenty of time for a chat and a gossip when we've found this missing tiara."

While the guards watched, Kate carefully searched through all my clothes.

"I haven't taken the tiara," I said.

"Of course you haven't," said Kate.

"Of course she hasn't," said Zapristi.

"Well, who has?" asked the taller of the two guards.

"I don't know," said Zapristi sadly.

Max gave a little squeak and scratched his head.

At five to ten, the guards marched us back into the small ballroom. The Happy Hendersons were already there, standing on the stage. 'Jolly Jim' Henderson glowered at Zapristi. Mrs Henderson blew her nose. The Henderson boys shuffled their feet nervously.

As the giant clock above the fireplace struck ten, the wide doors at the far end of the room swung open and in came the King and the Queen and the Princess Royal and little princess Alexandra.

"Well," said the King, turning to the guards. "Where is it?"

"We can't find it, Your Majesty," said the taller of the two guards.

"What do mean?" growled the King. "You can't find it? I don't believe it! Have you forgotten that I'm giving a hundred pound reward to whoever finds it?"

"We still can't find it, Your Majesty."

"Come on," said the King, narrowing his eyes and looking at the rest of us. "Own up. Which of you has taken the tiara?"

Nobody said anything, except for Max who ran forward squeaking loudly and suddenly pointed at 'Jolly Jim' Henderson.

The King laughed. "The marmoset seems to think it's you, Henderson. What do you say to that?"

'Jolly Jim' Henderson's red face grew redder, but he didn't say a word.

The King looked down at Max and chuckled, "Now my fine friend, if you find the tiara you get the reward."

Max clapped his paws happily and scampered across the stage to where 'Jolly Jim' was standing. With a quick tug he yanked 'Jolly Jim's Jolly Funny Hat Box' from out of his hand and ran with it straight to the King.

King Edward opened the hat box and there it was: Alexandra's beautiful diamond tiara, all safe and sound.

"Blast that monkey!" hissed 'Jolly Jim' Henderson.

"Arrest that man!" ordered the King.

Chapter Nine

"THANKS TO MAX"

So 'Jolly Jim' Henderson was arrested and taken off to prison, and the King of England was as good as his word and gave Max the hundred pound reward and a pat on the head.

"I should have guessed it was Henderson," sighed the Great Zapristi, examining the unstitched lining of his beautiful green cape. "What a rascal! I never trusted him. He didn't smell right."

I laughed. "He smelled awful."

"But how did he do it?" asked Kate.

"Easy!" said Zapristi. "'Jolly Jim' was on stage the whole time, remember. He planned it very cleverly. He was standing right by the back of the magic cabinet. The moment I closed the cabinet doors, all he had to do was put his hand in the back and pop the precious tiara into his silly hat box. By the time Maisie got round to the back of the cabinet, the deed was done. What a rogue! I'm sorry I ever met him."

"I'm not," I said. "If you hadn't met 'Jolly Jim' Henderson, we'd never have been invited to Windsor Castle and we wouldn't have met the King of England and, most important of all, I wouldn't have found my friend Kate again, would I?"

"Quite so," agreed Zapristi. "Maisie, the girl who lost her head turns out to be Maisie, the girl who found her friend. But I must say I don't quite understand how one minute Kate was on a boat bound for Canada and the next she's a ladies' maid at Windsor Castle."

"I got to Canada," Kate explained. "I went all the way, but I didn't stay for long. One day, on the boat going over, I was called to see the captain. He was a very kind man with a bushy brown beard who said, 'Young lady, I understand you don't want to go to Canada to be adopted by a nice Canadian family. Is that right?' I nodded. 'You'd rather go back to England, would you?' I nodded again. 'Can you sew?' I nodded and said, 'Yes, sir.' 'Good,' he said. 'That's what I hoped you'd say, because I happen to know there's a very grand lady on board who is looking for an assistant ladies' maid and you might just be the girl she needs.'

"I was. Lady Bullimore turned out to be a lady-in-waiting to the Queen. She was going to Canada to visit her brother the Governor-General and,

after three months, she was coming back to England, to live at Windsor Castle and help look after the Queen. Lady Bullimore took me on, and she liked me, and I liked her, and here I am."

"What adventures we've all had," said Zapristi, smacking his lips.

"The best thing about our adventure," I said, looking at the Great Zapristi, "is that it has a happy ending – thanks to Max. He's told me we can all have a share of the reward. That means you get twenty-five pounds, Zapristi!"

The Great Zapristi clapped his hands with joy. "You mean I can afford the fare to go back to America?"

"You can," I said, "but you can't go yet."

"Why not?" He looked worried.

"Because first I want you to show Kate how you chop off my head—"

He laughed. "With pleasure, child."

"In fact, I want you to teach us all your tricks so

that one day we can earn our living as magicians."

"That's an excellent idea," said Zapristi. "I'll teach you everything I know and then I'll go back to America."

"No, then you'll be going on holiday."

"On holiday? Me? Where?"

"On a boat," I said.

"With us," said Kate.

"On our boat, in fact."

"But you haven't got a boat," said Zapristi, looking very confused.

"Not yet, but with Max's reward we're going to get one. And you're going to help us find it and buy it and paint it. It's going to be all yellow and red and green. We're going to have our very own barge on the river Thames and live happily ever after. Never look back, only look ahead. Remember?"

Zapristi smiled and said, "Mr and Mrs Noah

89

would be very proud of you, my girl. What will this boat of yours be called?"

"The good ship *Max*, of course!"

Max gave a happy squeak and jumped up into my arms.

Zapristi looked at him and laughed. "Isn't he the most amazing monkey?"

"No," I said. "He isn't a monkey, he's a marmoset."

MAX, THE BOY WHO
MADE A MILLION
by Gyles Brandreth

*"You're going to have to be brave, boy —
brave and strong."*

When Max's father is arrested for something he
didn't do, Max runs away and joins up with the
Great Zapristi — Master of Illusion — Famous the
World Over! Max *must* clear his father's name
and earn enough money to get him out of prison.
Dare he do it as Maximilian Rich, the Boy Who
Walks the Tightrope? Max's riproaring
adventures take him from the streets of 1890s
New York to the Niagara Falls — through lions'
cages, storms at sea and dazzling feats of bravery.

*Another Collins Red Storybook
to add to your collection!*

Collins
An Imprint of HarperCollins*Publishers*
www.**fire**and**water**.com

THE WITCH'S TEARS
by Jenny Nimmo

In freezing hail and howling wind, a stranger is given shelter at Theo's house – a stranger who loves telling stories and whose name is Mrs Scarum. Theo is convinced she's a witch and wishes his father would return home from his travels. But the blizzard continues and the night is long... and there may be tears before morning.

Another Collins Red Storybook
to add to your collection!

Collins
An Imprint of HarperCollins*Publishers*
www.**fire**and**water**.com

HARRY THE POISONOUS CENTIPEDE
by Lynne Reid Banks
Illustrated by Tony Ross

Harry is a poisonous centipede, but he's not very brave. Still, he is the star of this *seriously* squirmy story. Harry likes to eat things that wriggle and crackle, and things that are juicy and munchy. But there are some things that a poisonous centipede must never try to eat – dangerous things like flying swoopers, belly wrigglers, furry biters and the most dangerous of all... *Hoo-Mins*.

Another Collins Red Storybook
to add to your collection!

Collins
An Imprint of HarperCollins*Publishers*
www.**fire**and**water**.com

Order Form

To order direct from the publishers, just make a list of the titles you want and fill in the form below:

Name ....

Address ....

....

....

Send to: Dept 6, HarperCollins Publishers Ltd, Westerhill Road, Bishopbriggs, Glasgow G64 2QT.

Please enclose a cheque or postal order to the value of the cover price, plus:

UK & BFPO: Add £1.00 for the first book, and 25p per copy for each additional book ordered.

Overseas and Eire: Add £2.95 service charge. Books will be sent by surface mail but quotes for airmail despatch will be given on request.

A 24-hour telephone ordering service is available to holders of Visa, MasterCard, Amex or Switch cards on 0141-772 2281.

Collins
An imprint of HarperCollinsPublishers